NEVER MAIL AN ELEPHANT

BY MIKE THALER
ILLUSTRATED BY JERRY SMATH

HB
HINKLER
BOOKS

For all the wonderful gang
at the Stone Ridge Post Office, 12484.
M.T.

For the hard-working people at the
Croton-on-Hudson Post Office, 10520.
J.S.

Never Mail an Elephant
Published in 2003 by Hinkler Books Pty Ltd
45-55 Fairchild Street
Heatherton Victoria 3202 Australi
www.hinklerbooks.com

10 9 8 7 6
10 09 08

In association with BridgeWater Paperback.

Previously published by BridgeWater Paperback, an imprint and
trademark of Troll Communications L.L.C. in 1998.

978-1-8651-5974 4

Printed and bound in China.

One day I decided to mail my cousin Dilly
an elephant for her birthday.

So I went to the stationery store
and got lots of wrapping paper.

Then I went to the hardware store
and got a big ball of string.

Next I emptied my piggy bank and went
to the post office to get lots of stamps.

Then I went to the zoo and got an elephant.

I covered the elephant with wrapping paper,

wound it round with string, and tied a bow.

Then I addressed it.
The elephant giggled because it tickled.

I let my dog Lucky lick the stamps.

Then I pasted them on.

Lucky's tongue stuck to the floor.
I pulled him loose.

Then we put the elephant on my wagon...

TO DILLY DUMPLING
321 WEST CHESTNUT ST.
HI HO, OHIO. 0000

MAIL MAIL

and pulled it to the corner mailbox.

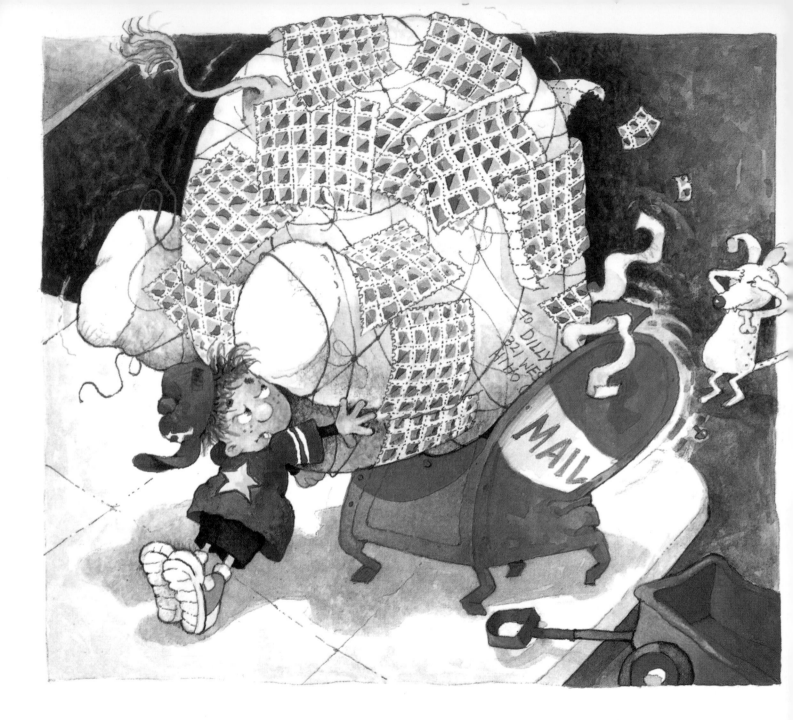

Then I pushed...and shoved...

and stuffed the elephant in!

As I headed for home I met the mailman

and told him about the elephant.

The mailman went to the mailbox
and opened the door.

Then he pulled...and tugged...

...and yanked the elephant out!

Then he wrestled it onto his cart

and putted slowly to the post office.

The postmaster put the elephant on the scale.
Then he stamped it!

The elephant went WILD!
Its legs shot out of the wrapping paper.

It jumped into the air, crashed through the wall...

...and ran all the way back to my house.
Since Dilly's birthday was that afternoon,
I did the next best thing I could do...

I tied a pink ribbon around the elephant.

Then Lucky and I climbed on top

and rode it next door to her party.

Happy birthday!